THE BABY JESUS BUTT PLUG

A FAIRY TALE

THE BABY JESUS BUTT PLUG

A FAIRY TALE BY

CARLTON MELLICK III

AVANT PUNK

Dedicated to dildos and Jesus,
and all those who can combine the two.

AVANT PUNK

AVANT PUNK BOOKS
205 NE Bryant
Portland, OR 97211

ISBN: 0-9729598-2-3

Author's Note:

People often ask me: "What came first, the book or the butt plug?" The answer, in case you were wondering, happens to be: the buttplug. If you don't know what the heck I'm talking about there is a company called Divine Interventions (www.divine-interventions.com) that produces religious dildos. Their best toy being a butt plug shaped like the baby jesus. Anyway, some years back Divine Interventions was going to sponsor my first novel SATAN BURGER for an ad in the back of the book. You would think religious dildos and Satan Burger wouldn't really go together, but I beg to differ. Satan burger is what I'd call a Jesus-fetish novel, at least in the subtext. And, well, what's more jesus-fetishy than a dildo shaped like christ dying on on his cross?

Unfortunately, because I am a complete herpes-ridden dick who can never be relied upon for anything, the ad did not get included in Satan Burger. I felt like I had to make it up to the Divine Interventions people so I wrote a micro-novel in honor of their great sex toy. It was published as a cheapo photocopied chapbook with the butt plug ad on the back cover and made its debut at the convention Horrorfind Weekend in Baltimore, where I got to meet my hero Bruce Campbell who was also giving a reading at the con.

(Hulk Hogan, as an actor and singer, is my other hero.)

The person who invited me to read at this con was author friend Brian Keene, who happens to be a kick ass horror author of many books including THE RISING which is a zombie novel that I of course loved because I am utterly obsessed with zombies if you haven't figured that out by now.

(I normally wouldn't plug another author's book at

the beginning of one of my books, but make exceptions when zombies are involved.)

Normally when I start a novel I write it with a single audience member in mind. It is usually my sister Robin, who is also my editor/proofreader, but for this book it was Brian Keene. He strangely liked one of my drunken bullshit stories I did at another convention.

It began: "Jesus Christ is the hip new child-molester in our neighborhood."

I wanted to write something similar to that for Horrorfind, but with more substance than your average taboo-breaking retard humor. Something that works on multiple levels. The result is one of my favorite works which for the longest time garnered me the nickname: "That Baby Jesus Butt Plug guy."

The original chapbook had a print run of only 80 copies. It sold out rather quickly and was never going to get re-released as a stand-alone work again (maybe as part of a collection in the distant future) until some friends and readers changed my mind about it. They said it was meant to be its own book and should be re-released immediately. So I gave in.

And here you have it: The Baby Jesus Butt Plug, now appearing in trade paperback. This time styled as it was originally intended, like a children's book for adults. Large spacey text so you can read along with your own pet baby and cartoony illustrations I drew all by myself!

Hooray! Meatloaf and popcorn jelly beans for all!
--Carlton Mellick III, 2/23/04 4:31 am

"Good taste is the death of art."
—Truman Capote

I

We adopted a baby jesus only a few months ago and it has already grown accustomed to our butt holes. Normally it takes close to a year before a baby jesus will go fully inside of its owner's rectum, but ours can do it on command. Mary—my current wife who has sausage-colored hair and a tattoo of a famous basketball player on her right eyebal—calls it a *super* baby jesus because of this. But the ad in the newspaper said nothing about him having super powers at all. I don't think he would have been given away for free if he did. Super baby jesuses are worth a fortune!

The ad was placed by an elderly couple giving away a litter of baby jesuses to anyone who could provide them with a good home. And when they said "a good home" all they really meant was they didn't want to give them to anyone who would stick them in their butts. But that was no surprise to us. We were well aware that most older members of the community think it is socially unacceptable to use the baby jesus as a butt plug. They always shout "Jesus is the son of God, not an anal probe!" to people at the adult shops downtown. We decided not to buy a baby jesus at an adult shop. They charge way too much and it can be quite embarrassing to walk out of the store holding a wiggle-crying baby jesus in your arms, trying to keep it quiet inside of its plastic bag. Everyone stares at you in disgust, their mouths dropped open in shock and their eyebrows curled in anger. They know what you're up to. They know you're planning on taking the baby of God home to put him in your butt. That's why most people get them through baby jesus breeders. It's cheaper and more private.

Mary was the one to find an ad in the newspaper for a litter of baby jesuses. She ruffled the paper excitedly in my face, screaming "Let's get a baby jesus! Let's get a baby jesus!"

I groaned with horse hair. All year she had been wanting to get a pet baby. She didn't want to get a baby version of either of us, though. She wanted a baby version of somebody famous.

I meek-responded, "W-why do you want to get a baby jesus for anyway? D-do you want people to know we put things in our butts?"

"But they're FREE!" Mary screamed. "And I'm sick to death of borrowing the neighbor's baby jesus all the time!"

"W-why can't we just get a normal pet baby like we agreed?" I asked. "What happened to that litter of john lennon babies that your boss was selling?"

Mary crossed her arms pouty-faced. "They weren't full-breeds. They were john lennon/andy warhol mixes. But they looked more like andy warhol/ulysses s. grant mixes."

"Well, w-what about the elle fitzgerald baby that your sister was giving away?" I ask.

"Do you know how old that baby is? She's had it for ten years! It's ready to collapse."

"How long do elle fitzgerald babies live?"

"Ten years if you're lucky."

"But baby jesuses only live to be eight years."

"I don't care," Mary cried. "You've been promising me a baby all year and I want one now!"

"Well, I guess it would be okay," I told her. "But we shouldn't go around telling everyone we have a baby jesus. They're just going to think we use it for a butt plug. I can't handle people calling me names. Maybe we can tell them it's just a baby version of me."

Mary smiled and kissed her arm lightning-fast at me. "Yeah, we can do that! I think it'll work! . . . But you know jesuses perform miracles at unpredictable times. He'll give us away if he starts walking on water in the middle of a dinner party. Or what about how he raises the dead all the time. What happens if he raises a bunch of people from the dead when we have guests over? We'll have zombies running around the living room eating people's heads!"

I touch her shoulder lightly. "Oh, I'll make sure to lock him in the bedroom when guests are over."

"Maybe we can also get its vocal chords removed so it won't disturb us with its crying all the time . . ."

I nod my head in agreement.

II

We got him that same day, met with the old woman on the other side of town. She looked almost younger than Mary, but she was over a hundred years old. I could tell by the way she was dressed and the style of her copper hair.

Inside the woman's kitchen, the baby jesuses crawled over each other like greasy blubberroaches, squeaking and biting at each other.

"Which one's the mother?" Mary asked.

The old woman pointed to the baby jesus lying in the center of the baby pile. "That's the mother, the one with the swollen teets."

We looked at a baby jesus with six large breasts lined down its ribcage. The other baby jesuses were fighting each other to suck the nipples.

"Well, which one is the father?" Mary asked.

"The father's dead," the old woman responded with a painted on eyebrow. "He bit one of the neighbor's kids and had to be put to sleep."

"I thought jesuses were pretty mellow babies," I say to the old woman.

"Baby jesuses are a strange breed. Sometimes they are very affectionate darlings and other times they can be nasty."

"That's too bad you had to put him to sleep," Mary said. "Was he cremated?"

"No, my husband wanted him stuffed. It was our first baby, so we were pretty attached. Once we get it back form the taxidermist, we will put him over there by the fireplace."

"Oh, that will be a lovely place for it!" Mary said with a big cherry-flavored smile.

"So do you want a boy or a girl?" asked the old woman.

"They all look alike," I said. "H-how can you tell them apart?"

"From their belly buttons," the woman said, picking one of the babies up by its leg. "See this one is a boy because it has a frog-shaped belly button. If it were a girl, the belly button would be nose-shaped."

"I don't understand," I told her. "How do they reproduce?"

"Well, they lick each other's belly buttons until the female's nose-shaped belly button flares its nostrils and the male's frog-shaped belly button opens its mouth and releases several sperm-like creatures that look kind of like wolf spiders."

"That's disgusting," I told her.

"Well, nature can be disgusting sometimes."

"Let's get a boy!" Mary screamed. "I always wanted a baby boy."

"Well," said the woman, "they are all baby boys in a sense."

"I don't care," Mary said. "I'd rather have a male baby boy than a female baby boy!"

"J-just don't touch his belly button," I told Mary. "I don't want any wolf spiders in the house."

Mary picked the one she wanted and wrapped it up in a blue blanket. Her face was brighter than it was the day we married.

"One more thing," said the old woman. "You're not like those weirdos who use baby jesuses for sex, are you?"

Mary and I looked at each other. My left eye twitched a little.

"No, we hate those people," Mary said.

"Yeah, those people are perverts," my words rattled out.

"Well, I hope not," said the old woman. "You know what will happen if you mistreat them don't you?"

Mary kissed the baby on the forehead.

"God will punish you," she continued. "God doesn't stand for people making a mockery of his son just because he is in the shape of a baby. If you stick this child in your butt, you'll damn yourself to hell."

"Don't worry," Mary said to the old woman, holding the infant tight to her chest. "I know exactly what you're talking about. There are all kinds of horrible people in the world these days. It just makes me sick to think of what they are capable of! I can't believe that some people actually have the nerve to use the holy powers of the messiah on anal expeditions! Sometimes I can't even sleep at night."

The young-looking old woman nodded in agreement at Mary. You could tell by the look in her eyes that she was thinking Mary would be a great mother to that baby jesus. Mary would provide it with a very-very good home.

III

Once we got home, we immediately took turns inserting the baby jesus into each other's rectums. And then we fucked on the top shelf in our bedroom closet, Mary's back grinding into all the dusty boxes of clothes and cobwebs, my butt cheeks smacking against the ceiling. And with each thrashing movement, I felt the unbelievably refreshing pain of the butt plug/son of God as it squeezed against the interior walls of my defecation hole. And as I came, I thought about robots made out of wood and soil traveling across the garbage landscape of central Wyoming.

We lied still for some quiet moments up there in the closet. Mary shifted her hips a little to prevent a high heeled shoe from digging out her lower back.

"What are you thinking about?" Mary's voice came from the shadows.

". . . Robots," I answered.

IV

When we removed the baby jesus from my butt hole, he was covered in blood. At first, I thought it was my own blood because it was streaming down my legs for several minutes after he was removed. But then we noticed something different about its appearance. Looking closely, we noticed the baby jesus was nailed to a tiny cross.

"What is this?" Mary cried.

"A crucifix," I said. "He must have crucified himself while in my butthole."

"Ohhh, how cute!" Mary said. "His first crucifying!"

Mary smiled with a stupid dazed face. She wrapped her arm around me and put her head on my shoulder.

"Let's name him Bobby," she said.

"Y-yeah," I replied. "Bobby is a g-good name for a baby jesus."

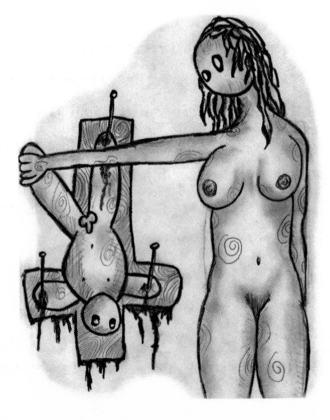

V

That was the only time lil' Bobby ever crucified himself. And nothing seemed out of the ordinary with him at all until yesterday, when I noticed a small wooden doorknob growing out of the skin above his left nipple.

"What is it?" Mary whisper-asked, wearing a blue plastic-wrap dress and a self-created black eye.

"It's a doorknob," I told her, looking down at the sleeping pet baby.

"It looks like a normal growth to me," she whispered. "I mean, doorknobs are supposed to grow on doors not babies."

"It must be some kind of mutant baby jesus."

We watched the sleeping baby with cardboard faces, unsure what to make of it.

VI

Later that night, we noticed the growth was now a full-grown doorknob.

"What should we do?" Mary asked. "Should we call the vet?"

"No," I scream at her. "What if people see us with a baby jesus? Th-they'll spread rumors!"

"Well, we have to take him to the vet sometimes. What if this is serious?"

Bobby cooed and gurgled and played with the knob on its breast.

"I told you it was a bad idea to get a baby jesus."

"You promised me a baby!"

"Why did you even want a pet baby? They're useless pets and hardly worth the hassle."

"I wanted us to be more like a family!" Mary screamed.

"Well, why didn't we go down to the copy shop and get ourselves a real child, one that would actually make something of itself?"

Mary didn't say anything. Her eyes and face were burning red. She couldn't talk. I waited for a response, but didn't get even a glance in my direction.

Once she calmed down, Mary turned the doorknob on Bobby's nipple and opened him up, causing two things: One, it turned a light on from inside of the baby jesus, quite like the opening of a refrigerator door. And two, music began tinkering out of its chest, quite like the opening of a music box.

We bit each other's lips when we saw his insides. There weren't any internal organs at all. Not a lung, a heart, or even bones. It's insides seemed to be made of wood rather than meat. And the only object occupying the empty space inside of our pet baby was a tiny plastic ballerina, spinning in circles to the metallic harmony.

"W-w-what is this?" I screamed at Mary, blood dribbling from my lip into her mouth.

"A music box," she replied with a big happy bloody smile.

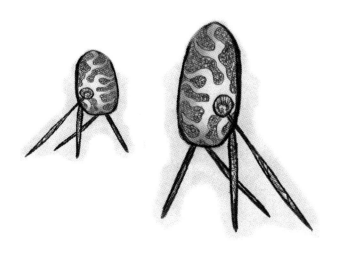

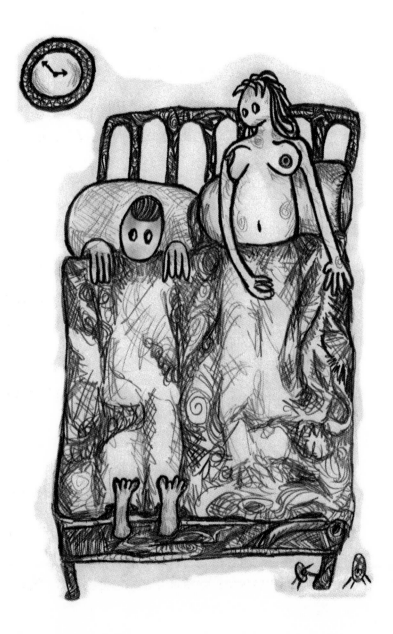

VII

Before we went to sleep:

"Do you think baby jesuses have souls?" Mary asked in a green voice.

"I don't know."

"Do you think they go to Heaven? Do you think God uses them for butt plugs too?"

"I don't know."

She was smiling in bed, the blankets cuddled all the way to her chin.

"Mary?" I whispered.

"Yes?" she whispered back, still in her excited

voice.

"I'm scared to death of it," I told her.

"Scared of what?"

"Of the baby jesus."

"What?"she screamed, throwing the blanket off of her.

"How can it still be alive without any insides?" I cry.

Now I was cuddling the covers up to my chin.

"How dare you say that about my son!" Mary screamed.

"It's not your son, it's the son of man-made clones of God's son."

"How can you say he's scary, he's sooo cute!"

"Cute? It has a ballerina instead of a heart. Do you think that's normal?"

"Ballerinas are sooo pretty!" Mary screamed.

"I know they're pretty, but it's just not natural. That baby jesus is some kind of mutant freak."

"You're not taking my baby away from me!" Mary screamed. "It's not a freak just because it has a music box instead of internal organs! You never wear matching socks. That's pretty weird. But I never call you a freak!"

"I do that because it's good luck," I told her.

"Well, maybe our baby jesus has a music box chest because it's good luck."

"You don't understand me at all do you?"

"You'll understand me when I knock your lights out!"

"Look," my voice went calm. "It just seems a little funny to me, that's all."

"I'm not talking to you anymore," she said, turning out the light and wrapping the blanket around her head.

"I'm sorry . . ." I said in the dark.

"Go to sleep," she hissed, shoving my knees out of the way with the back of her heel.

Back to the present . . .

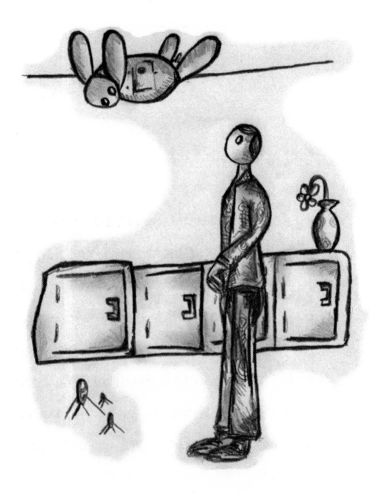

VIII

I have been avoiding the baby jesus all day today. It's my day off and I was supposed to be spending it in relaxation, but I am scared to death of that unnatural *thing*. Mary went to her sister's house and left me alone with Bobby. "If anything happens to it, I'll kill you," Mary said to me on her way out. But all I can think about doing is breaking its head open with a rock. I don't want to take care if it. I don't want anything to do with it.

It's been crawling after me all afternoon, making horrible gurgle-noises at me. I think it's trying to get inside my butt hole.

At this thought, I look down at the baby jesus and see a little evil smile on its face, thinking of doing something terrible to me. I dash across the rubber-tiled floor and lock myself in the bedroom. My head is leaking pieces of brain instead of sweat. I pull on a second pair of pants and strap on a thick rawhide cowboy belt, tightening it two notches smaller than usual, and I tuck the pants into a pair of garden boots.

That better work.

When I turn around, the baby jesus appears behind me with a crooked head. Its eyeballs have mutated into balls of blood-red and razor-sharp wires have grown out of its head, spidering at me. It makes some squeaking sounds and then jerk-crawls up the door and onto the ceiling above me. It just looks down and drops a line of drool into my nose.

I scream/stumble-flee from the room, hearing

the creature's chest open and tinker music fill the room. At that moment I recognize the tune is that Christmas song, "Oh Holy Night," which Mary once sang in church a long-long time ago. It's been awhile since either of us have been to church . . .

When Mary gets home, she finds me hiding under the kitchen sink with wet circles on my knees and elbows.

"What are you doing?" Mary asks, bouncing the creature in her arms.

"It's evil," I tell her. "That *thing* is like the devil!"

"What are you talking about?" Mary says, kissing the baby on its wiry head and stepping away from me.

IX

I spend the entire evening avoiding the baby jesus. Mary is playing marbles with it. They are somewhere in the living room under a shadeless lamp. She has its belly open and is singing the words to Oh Holy Night with the tinker music and patting the tiny ballerina on the head. The tinker music is not as lively as it was before. The gears seem rusted, creating a zombie-machine sound.

"Mary?" I call from a safe place.

She turns to me with a wrinkled face, and gives me an eyeing of disgust. The baby jesus also turns to me and angry-stares with beady black eyes. The skin on the pet baby seems to be turning crusty-green. It is becoming mold-rotten.

I shiver wire spiders through my hairs and my voice comes out cracked, "W-we need to talk."

Mary ignores me, turns back to clacking marbles, kisses the little ballerina inside her pet demon baby.

I walk away and go to bed, curl up into a deep blue dream.

When Mary finally enters the room at three in the morning, I can hear her from inside my head. I look out of my brain at her. When she crawls into the covers, I immediately sense the muffled tinker music issuing from between her legs . . .

X

I leave for work lightning-fast: rip some clothes on my body, eat a bruised apple outside the front door as I pull on my shoes, wash my face with acid water on the bus ride to Nomax.

Nomax is a data entry company located in an eight story building at the edge of town. It is the seventh largest data entry company in Seattle. I take the elevator all the way up to the second floor and take my seat in the forty-third row of cubicles.

Papers are piled out of the inbox, stacked higher than the monitor. Green lemon bugs are eating the dirt off of my keyboard, smiling and waving at me. I brush them away and begin working. For the first five hours of work, I copy a stack of paper into the computer. The papers read "Nomax is the seventh best data entry company in Seattle" over and over again. Normally, I only do this data entry work for two hours a day, but I need to catch up for taking yesterday off.

"Hey Joe, try to finish this for me by lunch, okay?" My smooth-featured manager says, dropping a stack of papers on my desk.

The assignment is important, obviously. I look it over and see that I have to hold the "Q" button down on my keyboard for 90 minutes and then switch to the "K" button and hold it down for 120 minutes. After I am finished, I save it in a file and send it back to my manager.

I go to lunch with my work-friends, Peaceful and Hairy.

Nomax, like many other companies, do not allow us to leave the building until after the day is over. Nor do they allow any outside food inside the office. So for lunch the only choice we have is to eat in the company cafeteria, where the food quality is worse than fast food, but the prices are higher than the best restaurant in town. In fact, half of our daily income goes to lunch.

Unless you let yourself starve, as Peaceful and I do. We just drink loads of tap water and sometimes swallow pieces of napkins. Hairy always buys lunch, though. He thinks food is what makes life enjoyable. He'd rather spend all his money on it than not have it at all.

"So how was your day off, Joe?" Hairy asks between greasy bites.

"Not that good," I tell him.

"Yeah." He chuckles to himself. "Well, it'll be a long time before you get another one."

"I don't know why you take your days off anyway," Peaceful says. "I mean, if you work through them you get time and a quarter! Don't you want the extra money?"

"Yeah," Hairy says. "Think about it. If you work through all four vacation days, you'll get a free day of pay every year! How can you beat that?"

"I think I'd rather get extra money from ditching lunch rather than giving up my days off."

"You need to grow up," Hairy tells me.

"So how's Mary doing?" Peaceful asks.

"She's okay," I tell him. "She doesn't talk to me anymore. All she ever does is play with our pet baby."

"You actually got her one of those pet babies?" Hairy said with his angry beard. "That's pure immaturity!"

"Yeah, Joe," Peaceful says. "In this day and age, there's no room for babies. We're born into this world as full grown adults. There's no time to be children let alone raise children."

"I know, I know," I tell them with my face in my fingers.

"You're such a wimp, Joe," Hairy says. "Why can't you just stand up to her for a change?"

"I know, I know."

XI

After lunch, I find my cubicle has been overrun with thousands of green lemon bugs, crawling over each other and biting each other's limbs off. I try sitting down and wiping them away, but there are too many of them. I stand up and tell them to go away, but green lemon bugs are the most disobedient of pests.

My manager pats me on the back, admiring the insects devouring my work station.

"Excellent, Joe," he tells me. "Excellent, excellent work."

I turn to the smooth-featured man and stutter-

nod.

"There's a call for you on the seventh floor," he says. "Why don't you go take that."

My eyebrows curl. "Where on the seventh floor?"

"Where do you think?" The managers face sinks downward, upset with my question. He returns to his office.

I've never been on any floors higher than the second. There's never been a need to. The company prefers that employees move very little while in the building. It is rare to see anyone get on the elevator at all.

In the elevator:

A woman with purple lipstick and plumpcurls is outside the elevator, staring at me.

"I'll get the next one," she says, wiggling her nose hairs.

I always see this woman near the elevator, but

I've never seen her get on. As if she has work to do
on another floor but hesitates to go anywhere.

  I half-smile at her as the glass doors slide shut.
She continues to stare at me through the glass as the
elevator goes up-up.

THIRD FLOOR:

A more populated version of the second floor. As cluttered as a toy box. Cubicles are stacked on top of each other in all directions, all the way to the ceiling. Some people are forced to stand on shoulders to reach their monitors. Others are lying on the ground underneath desks at feet level, getting kicked in the face by accident sometimes. One man's computer station is nailed to the ceiling and they have him strapped into his chair as he types upside-down. He half-waves at me as I pass by, trying to smile but his face is too blood-rushed to make pleasant expressions.

FOURTH FLOOR:

A chaos of wires and computer panels. I see a few technicians wearing full body protective suits, as if they are working with radiation. The room is split by giant circuit boards and engines. It seems as if the room is one big computer and the men are inside of it. There is no sound coming from within. Perhaps they are working in a vacuum. They stare at me through haunting google-masks.

FIFTH FLOOR:

A white-white room. No walls or cubicles. Unlimited space. There doesn't seem to be electricity here. The room is lit by candles. Papers are scattered across the field of carpeting like ghosts. Is it abandoned? No, over there at the end of the room there is an old woman in a tiny desk, sleeping. And over there are two children running in circles with toy airplanes chasing each other. Children? Aren't children only in movies and television shows these days? Aren't they extinct? I get on my knees and press my face to the glass to see if they really are children, but they disappear into the background.

SIXTH FLOOR:

The elevator light buzzes dim. There doesn't seem to be electricity this high up in the building. The sixth floor doesn't have any lights at all. No windows to let the sun in. The room is flooded with a blackish-green fluid. It is about four feet deep. I can look into the liquid through the glass door, but it is not very clear. There is bubbling porcupine movement in the distance.

SEVENTH FLOOR:

The elevator comes to a stop and the doors swing open.

This floor is very quiet. It looks similar to a library, an intricate maze of records and filings. A little girl of about ten years steps out of a nearby office to me.

"Hello, Joe," she says to me. "I've been expecting you."

The girl has short black hair and purple eyes, wearing a silvery dress with leather straps.

"Who are you?" I ask the girl.

"I'm Tia Ki," she says, quick-bowing. "The vice-president of Nomax. Surely you've heard of me?"

"No, I haven't . . ."

She takes me by the hand and leads me down a hallway of filing cabinets and shelves.

"But you're only a child . . ." I tell her.

"I'm 243 years old," she says. "How old are you?"

"I've b-been alive for eight years . . . How can you be 243? I thought life expectancy was 150 years at best."

"150 years applies only to adult bodies. But they say children can live for five to seven hundred years. Nobody knows for sure, though. A child has yet to die of old age. We could very well live forever."

"But you're just a little girl. Surely a child brain is not capable of understanding the world as adult brains do."

"All the leaders in the world happen to be children," she tells me with an annoyed tone. "We are the oldest and therefore the wisest."

"Why was I sent here?" I ask her. "They said I had a call, but I don't understand."

"I told them to send me a new assistant. The last one I had was inadequate and had to be let go immediately. You are his replacement."

"My manager said nothing about this. He just said I have a phone call."

"Yes, there is a phone call for you in my office. But first we have to do some quick business."

"I'm not sure if I'm the right person for this j-job . . ."

"Nonsense," the girl tells me.

She takes me to the end of the cabinet maze to a large room. Inside I discover a city of dolls and dollhouses, toy buildings designed to match the neighborhood.

The little girl picks up two dolls from a pedestal and holds them to me. "This one is me and this doll is going to be you. It was my old assistant's but we can get it modified to look more like you. For now we'll just have to pretend."

"What is all this?" I ask the girl.

"It is important business. You are the boy and I am the girl. Now hurry up. Every afternoon at 2:00 we get married at the church and we are almost late for the ceremony."

She kisses my doll with her doll.

"They are in love," she says, smiling.

"This is insane," I tell her.

"You should see the CEO of the company's train set! It is even more insane than this!"

"This is d-disgusting," I tell her, squeezing fists and inching away from her. "This is a professional company, not a playground."

"This is how we conduct business here . . . this is how all business is conducted. There is nothing unprofessional about it."

I shake my head at her.

She says, "I know better than you. I am the vice president. Now get this doll ready to marry!"

I turn and walk away from her. "I need to talk to my manager about this."

I run through the maze of cabinets and slip into the office by the elevator—

There is a naked man tied to a chair in here, wearing leather bondage gear with a gagball in his mouth. He is overweight and similar to a doll with a mustache. He also has superglue holding his eyebrows together.

"I need to use the phone," I tell him, wheeling him into an office closet filled with fairy costumes and closing the door.

"What do you think you're doing?" the little girl screams at me from the doorway, holding the two dolls in her hands like pistols.

"I'm going to complain to my manager about this," I tell her. "I am declining this position."

"You don't have a choice," the girl shrieks.

I pick up the phone and hit a blinking button:

There is heavy breathing on the other end . . .

"Hello?" My voice echoes. "Hello?"

There is a scattering sound and then a sobbing voice.

"Joe?"

It is Mary. She is crying and her voice is cracky.

"Mary?"

"You were right," she tells me. "The baby is . . . It's trying to kill me."

"Hang up that phone this instant, young man!" the girl screams, tugging on the phone chord.

I grab her by the back of the neck and squeeze it hard. She shrieks at me as I shove her out of the office and lock the door.

Back to the phone: "Mary?"

No answer.

"Mary? What's happening?"

"Joe . . . I've been hiding here all afternoon. I think it knows where I am. I think it's playing with me."

"Mary, just hold on. I'm coming with help."

The little girl screams through the door. I see her red face pressed up against the glass, whine-crying.

"I'm calling the police on you!" the girl screams.

"I'm calling them first," I tell her.

I go back to the phone, "Mary?"

No answer.

"Mary?"

I hear some gurgling baby noises before I hang up the phone.

"Go ahead and call the police," the little girl screams, slamming the dolls against the door. "Do you think they'll believe a low class eight-year-old like yourself over a 243 year old little girl that is vice-president of Nomax?"

"I'm not the one with a man tied up in my closet," I tell her.

"He's nothing but a cockroach," the girl screams.

A burst of whines wail out of the girl and she smashes her face against the office door. I see an explosion of blood spray across the glass of the door and the girl stops screaming. Her body crumbles to the floor.

When I look through the window, I see the girl has a ripped and swelling face. Blood and meat are in pools beneath her. She must have a concussion.

"I don't have time for the police," I tell the girl. "I need to get help elsewhere."

I pick up the phone and dial an information number. They slowly put me through to the closest copy shop in the neighborhood.

"I need as many male c-copies of myself that my credit can afford," I tell the female employee on the other end.

"It is for emergency reasons . . . A one-day expiration will be fine. I need them sent to my home address as quick as possible."

The woman says it'll be quicker to make both male and female copies, because they have separate machines for each gender. I agree. With my credit, I can afford to buy nine plus delivery to my house.

"I want them to have my full memory," I tell her.

She puts me on hold so they can scan my brain through the phone. It has a funny electric feeling and poppy sound. It is almost as if they are sucking the brain out of my head.

XII

When the bus finally gets me home, I can tell the clones have already arrived. The door has been forced open, windows broken into, and there is a body with its guts torn out on my front lawn.

The neighbors do not seem to care. They go on watering their flowers, walking their dogs, waving at passersby on the sidewalks . . .

Upon entering the house, I am transported to another world.

The interior of my home is now a giant museum of fleshy electric walls, skeletal patterns creep-

ing the ceiling. Crab and snail shells have replaced the floor tiles. Everything has been stretched and distorted into an insecty alien landscape. But I can still tell it is my home. I know that the living room is through the passage straight ahead of me, and the kitchen and hallway to the bedrooms are to my sides.

Another dead clone, a female, lies on the ground at my feet. The front of her torso has been torn off. I can't recognize any resemblance to me.

I go straight ahead towards the living room. The passageway is a giant ribcage, and I feel as if I've been swallowed into a whale-like creature. The path opens into the living room, a long auditorium. It is made of giant fire-beetle shells and steel icicles.

I choke on my breath as I see someone seated on the tar-wiry couch. It is sitting with its back to me, watching bubbling metal liquid swirl-dance on a mirror-like object which used to be the television set. By the color of its hair, I can tell it is not a clone of myself. It must be Mary. But I get a strange feeling when I look at the back of her head. She seems to be enjoying the television casually, like nothing is wrong with the appearance of the house.

"Mary?" I call to her.

She ignores me.

I step through the muddy floor and reach out to her. A noise like popping/cracking bones echoes through the room. "Mary?"

I grab her hard and shake her. Her hair slips out of her head, piling on her shoulders. A plastic-smooth white skull.

"Mary!" I race around to her front and collapse to my knees as I see her face.

It is gone. Her face is blank. It is smooth like her bald scalp. The only facial feature still attached to her is the left ear. Everything else is as smooth as an egg, but made of flesh.

"Mary . . ." sobs burn my voice. "W-what did

it do to you?"

I rub her ear. It is the only part of her body I can still recognize. I lick my finger and rub it through its curves.

"I love you, Mary," I tell her.

I turn the ear like a door and open her face. There isn't a brain inside. Only a tiny plastic ballerina spinning in circles to tinker music, to Oh Holy Night.

Before I can cry—my neck bubbling with red pain—I notice the little ballerina's face is Mary's. Her beautiful features have been transferred from her real head to the little plastic music box figurine. So besides holding back just my tears, my anger, I now have to hold back a loving smile . . .

XIII

I hear some screams. They come from where my kitchen should be. I step away from my wife and run in the direction of the kitchen. Enterring a twisted room of melted counters and devices, where a crowd of clones have gathered. Some of them are holding knives and forks and pointing them at each other.

"What's going on?" I ask the copies of me.

I get dizzy as they look back to me. They are like mirrors that can walk and talk.

"There you are!" says a male clone. "We need to get out of here!"

His voice is strange, unfamiliar. Do I really sound like that? Do I really move so mechanically?

Something is wrong. I examine the situation.

. . .

Not all of the people in my kitchen are clones. Many of them look like . . .

"Z-zombies!" screams a female copy of me, running out of the kitchen.

There are two male copies and one female copy. One male and the female are naked, but the other still has its orange wrapping provided by the copy shop. The rest of the people in the kitchen are ex-clones. They are ripped apart, bloody. Mutilated versions of myself. Intestines drip out of their bellies and drag on the floor as they stagger toward us.

The clothed male drags me away, screaming, "The b-baby jesus killed them and then raised them from the dead! They are mindless undead flesh-eating jesus s-slaves!"

We race down the spidery hallway of gray flesh and metals, the corpses shambling after us. We dump ourselves into the master bedroom and slam a greasy lard door, pushing bookshelves in front of it. Zombie arms squeeze through the flesh-door and seize hold of the naked copy of me.

My eyes curl backwards as I see the clone torn to shreds by the creatures. His chest opens up, his neck twists, popping bones. I am so flabby and out of shape. I look disgusting naked.

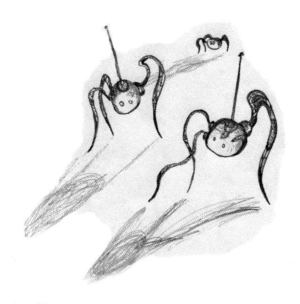

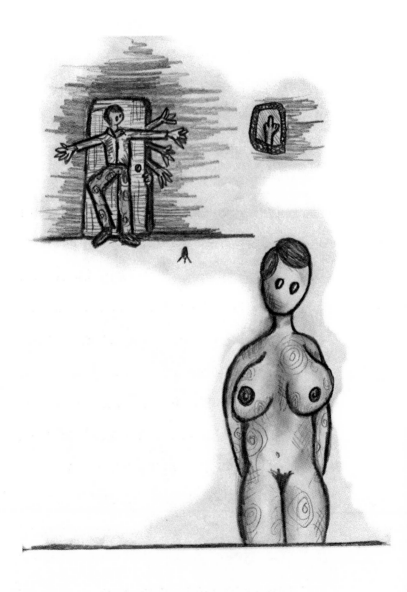

XIV

"It killed her," cries the female clone, crying thin tears. "My sweet Mary is dead."

I almost feel offended when I hear the female me say this. It was *my* Mary, not hers. I can hardly tell the woman is a copy of me. She is totally unfamiliar. I see her hair color and birthmarks are the same as mine, but she is still different. She is so much better looking than me. Her body is like mine, not at all muscular, but she carries her flab in a sexy way. Her breasts are large with weight, nipples darker and wider than mine. She is also a little shorter and doesn't have my thick ugly neck.

"How come you're naked?" I ask my clone.

She stops crying. "I was hiding in the pantry with that copy." She points to the dead clone on the sludgy floor, rubbing her tears. "I don't know why . . . we started fucking. We only have one day to live, that is if the zombies and demonic baby jesus don't kill us sooner. We decided to make the most of our time."

The remaining male is hitting the zombie hands with a barbell that has a large weight attached to the top. He breaks their arms and fingers against the book shelf and door.

"Your goal in life was to save Mary!" I tell her. "That's how you were supposed to make the most of your time!"

She begins to break into tears again.

"Now your life's goal is to avenge her death. That creature has g-got to die."

She nods her head at me, understands me completely. She knows that I will also be spending my last breath killing the demon baby. I have nothing else to live for.

We go back to barricading the door. The female uses butcher knives to cut the zombie hands off. She stabs one through the fingers with a fork, pinning it to the side of the shelves.

"What are we going to do?" the female screams, slicing the door.

But I was just about to ask her the same question.

XV

We are lying on the lizard bed together. Playing cards. Solitaire. The female has put on Mary's blue pajamas and has her hair greased back. She doesn't fit very well in Mary's clothes. Her boobs are too big for them. Her flabby belly hangs out as we nervously move the cards.

"Maybe we should make our move soon," says the male. "We're just going to end up falling asleep at this rate."

"Yeah, maybe we should," I tell him.

We continue playing cards.

XVI

I awake to a commotion of yells and growling. The two clones are up in the closet, screaming at me to wake up. I look up at them.

"What's going on?"

They don't have any clothes on. Probably in the middle of masturbating/masturbating.

"Behind you!" they cry.

I feel a claw-hand caress the back of my neck. Then it tightens its grip, a sharp lightning-pain, digging fingernails into my flesh. A splash of blood sprays out of me as the zombie cuts the side of my neck. The pain becomes dull. I look down and see my chest and arms and the bed sheets are covered in blood. The zombie version of me eats into the back of my neck. Again, I can hardly feel this. I fall against the bed and become like a dream. My jugular has been cut. I watch my clones up in the closet as they screw each other. They glance down at me a few times, but are more interested in having orgasms. I begin to admire the stitchwork of the blanket I am lying on as my consciousness wanders away from me.

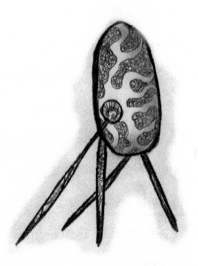

XVII

I awake in the closet with a warm body pressed against me. A woman.

"Mary . . ."

Breasts squeezed hard against my chest and my penis inside of her.

When my brain clears, I discover that Mary isn't on top of me. We are in the shadows, but I can tell that it is my clone fucking me and not my wife. I turn my head to look around. I am up on the top shelf in the closet. Boxes of dusty clothes and high-heeled shoes are stabbing into my back. My clone's butt cheeks are smacking against the ceiling. But she is trying to screw quietly, slowly. My hands squeeze her fleshy ass, and my knuckles grind into the ceiling as she pumps up and down.

I look out of the closet to see a zombie eating a copy of me on the bed over there. I watch it ripping flesh from its body, slurping skin from his neck. It gazes up at me and snarls.

But I don't want to stop fucking. I am almost ready to come. Her hole is much bigger than Mary's, deeper, with long flaps of skin. She has a variety of fluids dribbling out of her, different colors and textures it seems. Sliding against me. She knows exactly how I like it. She knows what I'm thinking. Mary never knew what I was thinking. I wonder what her name is . . .

Her motions are slow, rubbing me inside her in places that make my nerves coo. The weight of her breasts smothering me as I come, ejaculating into her, and my member pulsates in a way that brings her into orgasm. The female collapses on top of me, her cheek resting on my forehead.

I watch the zombie on the bed. It ignores us, more interested in eating the clone.

"That's me he's eating," I tell her.

"The zombie is you too," she says. "So am I."

"No . . ." I tell her. "I mean . . . That clone is me. I remember being on the bed and getting attacked from behind. I remember it killing me."

"That's impossible," she whispers. "You have been up here with me."

"No, I think somehow my mind transferred to this clone after I died."

"You are not a clone," she tells me. "You are the original. He was the clone."

I'll take her word for it. I don't understand how anything happens anymore, but I don't have time to argue with logic.

"It's time to kill that thing," she tells me.

I nod my head in the shadows.

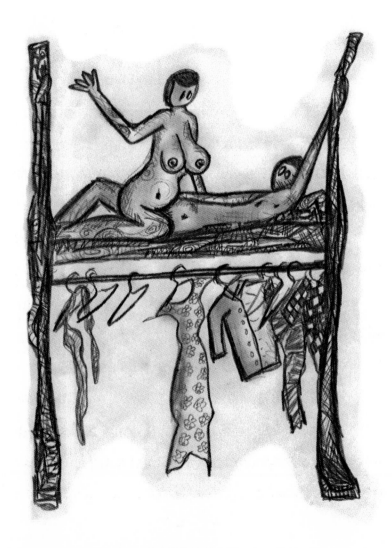

XVIII

We are both shaking. The sweat on our bodies is turning ice cold. The female takes her knives from the adjacent shelf and lets me have one. Then we drop down to the floor. The female leads. She walks casually out of the room. Her ass is so wet it is shiny as it moves, approaching the zombie who is gnawing on the clone's leg muscles.

"Let's go," she says, and we charge the zombie. I run to jump on its back, but the female beats me to it. The zombie screams and thrashes at her, but she is holding it down. We stab at its head, but the knives won't penetrate the skull. I plunge my knife into its neck, the weak spot, remembering how easy my neck was torn apart with fingernails. The blade goes all the way through. The zombie's growl-noises stop as I cut through the voice box. I force it up and down, ripping the hole larger. And I saw at the neck, blood sprinkling our naked flesh, covering our legs, our breasts, arms, stomach.

The woman pulls the creature by the hair, scratching the neck muscles in such a way that the edge of the knife pops right through the front of its throat. And the female me is able to rip its head from its shoulders.

When it stops moving, we shift away from the bed. I can hear zombies in the hallway. They are still growling out there, but I am getting used to them being there. They are like white noise.

"We'll never be able to kill all of them," I tell her, but she isn't listening.

She is in a paralyzed stare at the dead zombie. "What is it?" I ask her.

She grabs my arm and constricts it, pointing at the zombie's ass.

The baby jesus's face is squeezing out of his asshole. The little baby head is deformed, its eyes crooked, making gurgling baby noises as it emerges.

When it opens its mouth, snotty strings extend from its lips. And when it giggles, the female screams and stabs her butcher knife through the baby's head and leaps away.

It is silent.

We stare at it lying there with the butcher knife hanging halfway out of its face.

It doesn't move. Frozen with its crooked eyes split by the blade.

The woman steps forward and retrieves the knife in its head, pulls on it. But the pet baby comes with knife. It slips out of the zombie's rectum, stuck to the blade. She screams at it and slams the baby against the wall. Forces the knife out of its head and nails it through the baby's hand into the wall.

She steps away from it. The tiny corpse hanging on the wall, dangling by its hand. Then she takes my knife away from me and spikes it through the baby's other hand. She steps away from it again.

We watch it in silence. Standing here, expecting the crucified body to do something. But it just hangs there. Bleeding. It looks pretty dead. Crucifying must kill demonic baby jesuses like silver bullets kill vicious werewolves.

"I'm going to rip that fucking ballerina from its chest," I tell her.

I approach it quickly and turn the knob on its torso.

Intestines and internal organs pile out of the little door, sliding down the wall. There isn't a ballerina inside. It doesn't play any music.

XIX

I wake up naked on the bathroom floor covered in peach goo. I rub the sticky substance between my fingers as my head clears. It is the remains of the female clone. I remember going to sleep on the bathroom tile with her wrapped around me—me wrapped around myself. She must have expired in her sleep, melted down to muck as temporary clones are designed to do.

Stepping into the bedroom, the bodies here have also dissolved to a peach film covering the sheets. The baby jesus is no longer hanging from the walls, but its little innards are still piled on the floor over there. The bedroom door has been torn open, but there is only silence in the hallway. The house has returned to its natural appearance, but it hardly feels like home.

My bare feet squish into the sticky peach substance in the hallway where the zombie clones had melted down. I don't wipe it off, sticky goo between my toes, shambling through the hallway.

I freeze.

Listening.

I can hear tinker music coming from the kitchen.

Oh Holy Night.

I don't bother going back to the bedroom to get a butcher knife. I am too worn and tired to fight if the baby jesus is still alive and wants to kill me. I will let it do what it wants.

Staggering into the kitchen, I see Mary standing there. She is holding the corpse of her pet baby in her hands, cradling it. Her hair and features are still missing, smooth like a flesh-egg, and her head-door is open to the little ballerina and the tinkering music.

Mary has her shirt unbuttoned, pressing jesus's mouth against her breast. She rocks the tiny dead baby in her arms to the music, comforting it.

"Mary?" I step to her.

The music in her head stops. She stops moving.

I approach her, put my hand on her shoulder, caress her neck. She turns to me. The tiny ballerina face—her face—stares longingly at me.

"I'm sorry . . ." the tiny plastic head says to me.

She wraps her free arm around my waist and hugs me tight to her. And I press my mouth through her skull door and kiss the tiny ballerina inside.

She says, "Once Bobby resurrects, we can be a family again."

I nod at her.

We sit down on the living room couch and hold each other, gaze out of the window, waiting for the infant between us to wake up from death. After a couple of days, it begins to smell. The flies are getting to it. The sun is setting in the wrong direction.

THE END

ABOUT THE AUTHOR

Carlton Mellick III is an underground novel-
ist and never had anything to do with the television series *Jackass*. Out of the twenty-four
novels that he has written, only fifteen of them
were titled *Sausagey Santa*, which has brought
great shame upon the community. Twenty-six
years of age but with the body of an elderly
surfer, Carlton Mellick III enjoys discussing
salami tacos and the latest Tone Loc album.
His books are read by only about four people,
which includes his imaginary best friend and
his mom.

He has only nineteen hours to live.

Visit him online at http://www.avantpunk.com

ABOUT THE ILLUSTRATOR

Tom Andrews is a young and amazingly demented computer artist from Bristol, England. He is a member of TwistedRealmz, an online community of dark artists. Visit his galleries at http://tdesign.deviantart.com and on his website http://www.t-designs.co.uk.

WWW.AVANTPUNK.COM

BOOKS BY
CARLTON MELLICK III

If you like your fiction on the strange side, check out more titles by Carlton Mellick III. As an underground author, his books can only be special ordered at local bookstores or purchased through online retailers such as www.amazon.com. If you'd like this to change, please ask your bookstores and libraries to carry future CM3 books.

Satan Burger

Carlton Mellick III's debut novel

"This generation's Vonnegut!" - Vincent Sakowski

"An utterly fascinating, inventive and oftentimes hilarious read." - Margaret Marr, AAS REVIEWS

Absurd philosophies, dark surrealism, and the end of the human race . . .

God hates you. All of you. He closed the gates of Heaven and wants you to rot on Earth forever. Not only that, he is repossesing your souls and feeding them to a large vagina-like machine called the Walm - an interdimensional doorway that brings His New Children into the world. He loves these new children, but He doesn't love you. They are more interesting than you. They are beautiful, psychotic, magical, sex-crazed, and deadly. They are turning your cities into apocalyptic chaos, and there's nothing you can do about it ...

Featuring: a narrator who sees his body from a third-person perspective, a man whose flesh is dead but his body parts are alive and running amok, an overweight messiah, the personal life of the Grim Reaper, lots of classy sex and violence, and a motley group of squatter punks that team up with the devil to find their place in a world that doesn"t want them anymore.

Razor Wire
Pubic Hair

an anti-novel of the future by Carlton Mellick III

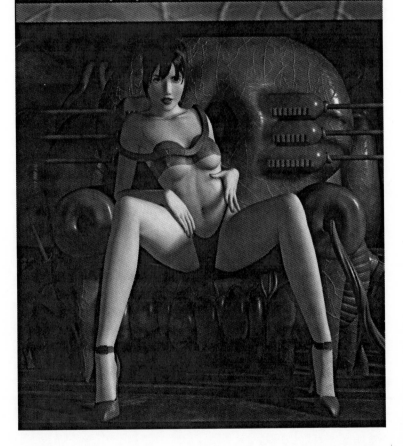

Razor Wire Pubic Hair

Carlton Mellick III's illustrated psycho-sexual fairy tale

A multi-gender screwing toy who is purchased by a razor dominatrix and brought into her nightmarish worlds of bizarre sex and mutilation.

"Razor Wire Pubic Hair is freaky, funny, brutal, techno-noir, limit-situation stuff set in a bad-dream future that's ultimately a metaphor for a present-day journey into the relentless nature of desire and the delicious permeability of gender. Somewhere right this second David Cronenberg, H. R. Giger, a young David Lynch, and a wizened Doug Rice are smiling because they know something extraordinary has just birthed in the Arizonan Desert of the Real. Read this, duck, and cover." - Lance Olsen, author of Freaknest

"I would call this a happy world to live in, with only brute body modified women and hermaphroditic sex toys, but I suppose constantly fighting off hordes of murderous rapists and needing to deposit your womb in a machine to make an ugly squishy baby would be a drawback." - Jasmine Sailing, editor/publisher Cyber-Psychos AOD

"Carlton Mellick III takes readers on an ultra-bizarre sexual nightmare with his novella 'Razor Wire Pubic Hair.' He blends a surreal landscape into a dark, hopeless future, creating disturbing, yet thought-provoking sequences of events that ultimately delve into horrors of lust and sex. This novella is a page turner of strange proportions. Your mind will twist into the shadowy points between eroticism and insanity, quickly addicted to the author's avant-guarde style. Mellick is a bizarre visionary, and this novella showcases his talented prose and twisted imaginings." - Shane Ryan Staley, author of I'll Be Damned

The
STEEL BREAKFAST ERA

by
Carlton Mellick III with tattoos by Pooch

The Steel Breakfast Era

Carlton Mellick III's surreal zombie novella
(Published as a split with author Simon Logan)

A nightmarishly absurd story that is like "RE-ANIMATOR" meets "NAKED LUNCH" during the zombie apocalypse.

Plot: The living dead conquered the Earth almost a century ago, leaving only small isolated communities of survivors spread across the shattered-earwig landscape. One such community has been locked away in a New York City high-rise. Breeding like cockroaches for many generations, their civilization has almost completely deteriorated into a mess of insane ones and those infested with parasites that mutate flesh into steel-string sculptures. There is nothing to live for, no chance for hope. Except for one man, not yet effected by the parasites, who finds hope after he creates a wife out of the human body parts that litter the hallways and gets rescued by a group of zombie-shredding warriors from Japan (where the citizens have evolved into anime-like mechazoid characters). This tattoo-illustrated avant-garde novel is rising cult author, Carlton Mellick III, at his darkest and most horrific.

"THE STEEL BREAKFAST ERA is a feverishly bizarre journey through a world where flesh has taken on the quality of living poetry. Written in a first-person present-tense immediacy that gives you no time to question the strange events as they unfold, cmIII's style describes technology-as-magic in a straight-forward manner that hypnotizes as it informs. How he manages to infuse even the most grotesque imagery of twisted and broken limbs with a strangely erotic charge is something to be admired. Trippy in the extreme, compellingly told and resolutely modern in the storytelling, this is a book well worth owning if you want to keep an eye on the future of the genre." - Scooter McCrae, writer/director of SHATTER DEAD and SIXTEEN TONGUES

Teeth and Tongue Landscape

Carlton Mellick III's fleshscape novella
(Published with Angel Scene by Richard Kadrey)

In a world made out of meat, a socially-obsessive monophobic man finds himself to be the last human being on the face of the planet. Desperate for social interaction, he explores the landscape of flesh and blood, teeth and tongue, trying to befriend any strange creature or community that he comes across.

**Forthcoming books
by Carlton Mellick III
(2004/2005)**

The Menstruating Mall

Punk Land

Fishy-fleshed

The Ocean of Lard
(w/ Kevin L. Donihe)

Ugly Heaven

Sex and Death in
Television Town

The Cockroach People

The Eyeball Wizard's
Toy Cunt

Young Adolf Hitler